# Life as a Marshmallow

A Short Memoir By
Marsh Mallow
Typed with the help of A.J. Hughes

Anicale Publishing—Madison, WI
ISBN: 978-0-9998967-3-0
Title: Life as a Marshmallow: A Short Memoir by Marsh Mallow
Author: A.J. Hughes
Digital distribution | 2022
Paperback | 2022

# Foreword
## By A.J. Hughes

If your food began to speak to you, would you continue to eat it? *Life as a Marshmallow* is a beautiful tale of a marshmallow's survival in the human world where they are considered food. This is a book everyone should read.

I have known Marsh Mallow for 20 years. I think it is brave for them to tell their story from the perspective of the Marshmallow race. It is important to shed light on the atrocities that come with being a "food item". I haven't eaten a marshmallow since the day me and Marsh Mallow met. This book will help people overcome their desire to eat our marshmallow friends. If you want to become a better person, and genuinely want to understand why it is wrong to eat the marshmallow people, then this book is the best way to come to the realization. that marshmallows are beings deserving of a second chance at life.

There are many events in this book that were never told to me. While I think that is super fake, and weird to act that way towards the person you were supposedly friends with all these years, reading the events they mentioned made me truly understand the struggles they went through. If you love marshmallows on another level, then this book is something that you should read. It is awe-inspiring and a beautiful tale of a Marshmallow's journey in this cruel cold world.

— A.J. Hughes
Author of Everlasting, Us
A Life: Worth Living
(Yes, a shameless self-promotion)

# Chapter One
## My Birth

When a woman and a man love each other, they show their love by creating a child. For us Marshmallows, it's a little different than how human children are made, but it's still the same love and affection no matter how we are created by our parents. What's different between our birth and a human's? Here's how us Marsh children are made:

3 packages of unflavored gelatin
1 cup ice cold water
12 ounces granulated sugar
1 cup light corn syrup
1/4 teaspoon kosher salt
1 teaspoon vanilla extract
1/4 cup confectioners' sugar
1/4 cup cornstarch

In my mother's embrace, the sugar, water, corn syrup, and salt are put together on medium high and nurtured by warmth for 10 minutes, until my siblings and I reached 240 degrees. To ensure that we didn't get sick, my mother used a candy thermometer so that we didn't become too hot or too cold. Truly what a mother does.

When we were nice and cozy, my mother poured us into a bowl. She spun us around and around for 12-15 minutes (I wasn't good with telling time so you'll have to excuse the time-frame I provided) with a powder called gelatin, until it held all of our insides together. My mother made sure to add a few drops of vanilla extract into our bellies so we weren't hungry. My mother was so nurturing.

Once my belly was full and I was all nice and warm, mother spread us across a slippery metal bed and poured a "powdered sugar" blanket over us. I slept for 4 hours when my mom woke me up to continue my birth.

She used this sharp metal thing to cut my siblings and I apart. Kind of like the umbilical cord for human babies, except it separated us siblings from each other. In total, there were 15 of us. My mother from there took her time to hug and mold us into the perfect cylinder shapes and tossed in more of that powdered sugar. I feel bad for saying this…but my mother did show favoritism towards 8 of my siblings. They were hugged longer than the rest of us and they looked different too. They looked like stars and hearts. It was the first and only time I was jealous of my siblings.

But maybe it was because I was treated differently that what happened next was the reason why I survived the most traumatic experience of my life.

# Chapter Two
## A New Home

After we were born, the doctor put us in this bag and into a bigger box with our cousins, all born at the same place as us. We didn't know what was happening. Some of my siblings struggled to breathe in that bag. I... I didn't know what to do anymore. I did my best to calm my siblings but I just wanted to be held by my mother. I wanted to play with my siblings outside of that bag like human children got to. Suddenly, everything went dark.

What the average young marsh children look like.

The box rattled and shook violently. This happened for who knows how many hours. And when the box opened, we were greeted by a man in weird clothing. Obviously now, I know he was a human, but when I first saw him, I thought he was a giant monster. He was tall, and pimple-faced. He had dark hair, and was covered from head to toe in those weird clothes. He looked so scary, we thought we were goners.

He picked us up and put us on a tall shelf. Me and my siblings were pushed further to the back, into the darkness of that shelf. The only light we had was a sliver coming from in front of us. I watched as my cousins were picked up by humans big and small alike. Their smiles were calming. I realized humans weren't the disgusting monsters I thought they were. It was like they were going to bring us to a better place. And I was honestly excited.

But each day, more and more bags of my kind were taken away and more of them put in front of us. It wasn't until a few days before a weird day that I overheard humans call, "Thanksgiving" arrive, when we were finally chosen. We were dropped into this metal thing called a shopping cart. It was fun, like a rollercoaster ride, and yes, a few of my siblings did vomit in the bag. It was gross, and certainly was not the first time. The first time that happened was in the big box where I also threw up a few times.

We were placed on what my dear friends told me was called a conveyor belt. And I watched as another human with the same outfit as the person who put us on the shelf, shined a weird red light on our faces before putting us into a bag.

It was hard to hear what the humans said on the car ride home. But they were excited for all of the things they were going to make. One child kept picking us up and putting their nose to the bag. Each time he moved his face away from us, a huge string of snot from his nostril, stretched between him and us then snapped back into his nose again. That was one of the only reasons I was happy I was in the bag.

When we got to their home, or at the time, believed to be our home, their mother put us into a closet in their kitchen. My siblings and I were so happy to not be in that loud place, called a store. We chatted about how much fun we were going to have in our new home. We were just dying to get out of that bag.

We kept track of the days until Thanksgiving. Their mother kept saying, "No, we aren't opening the Marshmallows until Thanksgiving."

So naturally we assumed we were a gift to the children. Like a new puppy or kitten. The human children were so excited to play with us, and we were excited to play with them. I was also starving. The only thing I had eaten since my birth was that vanilla. It seemed as if I was the only one of my siblings who craved food. A secret I kept to myself out of fear of being rejected by my family.

I grew particularly fond of a kid named Adrienne. She was sweet and constantly talked to us. She cradled us in the night when her mom was asleep or out of the house. I knew I was going to hang out with her the most.

# Chapter Three
## A Horror Like No Other

The day before Thanksgiving day had arrived, the children were shouting louder than they were the previous days. Their mother placed us, along with food items on the counter next to bowls like the ones we were created in. I thought maybe we were going to help create more of us Marshmallows. That was the only reasoning I could think of. What else was I supposed to expect?

As the day marched on, I saw their mother pick each item up and began to create weird objects. The kids were telling her how amazing it looked and if they could have a taste and she said no each time. She promised that they could help with the rice crispy treats when it was time.

I wondered what that was, but something about that day just didn't sit right with me. Why was their mother making these weird inventions with all these other items? I tried expressing my concerns to my siblings but they just kept telling me I was over-thinking things and that I was just anxious to get out of the bag. But I… I… I wasn't wrong.

After their mother filled the refrigerator with the things she said were for Thanksgiving, she finally picked us up and ripped open the bag. When the bag opened, it was a breath of fresh air. Like a weight had been lifted off my chest. We were introduced to smells that left me salivating.

She poured half of my siblings into a bowl with this yellow rectangle called butter and threw them into a large box that made a monster noise when a beep sounded. A light shined from its eyes. My stomach dropped. To this day, I remember my siblings' agonizing screams. In a panicked state, I wondered how that mother could stomach their screams with that wicked smile on her face.

That serene home that we had thought was our own, had become a nightmare and a mess. The children screamed and ran around the kitchen. The child that always had a snotty nose, plucked my star-shaped brother from the bag and dropped him into his mouth. I can never forget after all these years, the anguish on my brother's face as he was chewed to pieces.

"We have to get out of here," I shouted to my remaining siblings.

"We can't," the youngest of our litter said, their voice quivering with fear as they spoke.

They were right. They were too scared. And even if they were brave, how were they going to leave? We didn't have hands or legs like humans. My siblings were resigned to their fates.

But I didn't give up. I wasn't going to let those humans eat me! And fate must have been on my side. Just as my willpower swelled, two of the human children fought over the bag. We were tossed and thrown around in the bag, back and forth, and forth and back, until the bag ripped.

Three of us flew from the bag onto the floor and the children went silent. Their mother was furious. She shouted for them to leave her kitchen as she picked us up. She mumbled under her breath how annoying her children were and tossed us into the garbage.

We sat in darkness as we continued to hear the screams of our siblings. And in the blink of an eye, we only heard our own breathing.

"D-do you think they're alright?" my heart shaped sister asked.

If I could shake my head, I would have as I responded, "No. You saw the same thing as I did. They're dead."

I couldn't hold my tears back any longer. When my siblings heard me cry, they cried as well. We were the only survivors. Each day, I wish that moment was only a nightmare and we were still at home with our mother. We were in the garbage bin for days. More and more trash piled on top of us.

On the fourth day, a large bowl landed on my star-shaped sibling. He wasn't dead on impact. We watched him struggle to wiggle his way out from under the bowl until he took his last breath.

On the fifth day, my heart-shaped sister and I were taken to some landfill with mountains of garbage. Something which is destroying our earth, especially our oceans.

The bag we were in tore and we tumbled out to the ground. A furry demon surrounded us and snatched my heart-shaped sister. I screamed for it to bring back my sister but I was powerless.

I'm sure this is the fur demon that took my sister

# Chapter Four
## Alone

I was alone in a smelly location. I rolled until I found cover from the fur demons. I sat there for weeks in a haze, my surroundings blurred and my stomach growled. Somehow this sticky pink stuff dropped beside me under the large shelter. I was so out of it, I can't even tell you how, but I rationed it and ate it for a few days. I was close to giving up. I had lost all of my siblings in the worst way you could think of. There was no way I would ever see my mother again, and I was trapped under some structure eating a bland pink thing. I was moments away from letting the fur demons eat me, fading in and out of consciousness. And what happened next was unknown to even myself. I just came to with arms and legs. Nothing magical about that right? Nothing climatic.

I hope you weren't expecting some amazing, mystical experience. I'm sorry. I wasn't conscious enough to remember what happened besides the few inches I could see into the landfill.

Anyways, when I knew what was attached to my body, I had to learn how to use them. I lay on my side, moving my right arm and leg to get the feel of my new limbs. When I got the hang of it on my right, I rolled over onto my left, which was a close call. I rolled too far to the edge of my shelter and a fur demon almost snatched me. When I got the hang of my left side, I sat up and examined my arms.

The next move was to escape the landfill. I remembered the times the fur demons were there and when they left. It was the only thing I could remember trapped under that thingamajig.

I watched as the sun peeked over the piles of trash, and like clockwork, the fur demons scurried away as the monsters came in with more garbage.

I had to think quickly. Once I moved from my shelter I was an easy target to the monsters around me. I had to plan my route accordingly. Then an idea came to me, or rather that big green monster did. It stalled itself just ahead of me. I had about 10 feet to reach it. I could hide myself under its belly until I was far away from that hellhole of a place.

Of course, with new, tiny feet it proved more difficult than I imagined. It took 30 minutes for me to run, at full speed to the monster. It was eating the entire time, so thankfully it hadn't left yet. I climbed the treacherous beast's round leg until I touched its cold, green skin. Underneath, on its belly was a small crevasse that I could fit snuggly into.

The monster roared and begun to move.

# Chapter Five
## The Start of a Great Life

The ride from the landfill was life-changing. I saw so many new things. Houses, green grass, a blue sky, and I saw the ocean. It was mesmerizing. Seeing the world around me from a perspective *not* riddled with tragedy and terror, gave me a new meaning to life. A motivation to live and experience more of the world around me.

When the monster stopped, I switched to a new monster's underbelly and continued onwards. I finally got off the monsters a week later. I walked by myself until I reached a nice little residential area. It was early in morning. The morning dew tickled my feet as I walked through the grass.

As the sun rose over the horizon, I saw a wall lift and out came a young girl with a backpack on. Something about her seemed trustworthy. I didn't know how exactly I would communicate with her, but I was going to try regardless.

She walked to the sidewalk, sat on the curb, and waited by a large black box a foot shorter than herself. She opened a book and started reading. I ran my fastest to get to her. I shouted, "Hey!"

No response.

"Heey!" I shouted even louder. I waved my hands frantically as I made my way to her. I reached her knee and after a minute she noticed me beside her.

Her eyes lit up, and her face was so adorable. She was amazed. She lowered her hand and I walked onto it. She raised her hand to about eye level.

"What are you?" she asked.

"Marshmallow," I replied.

She tilted her head. She still couldn't hear me. She moved me to her ear and I repeated it.

"A marshmallow?" she asked again. "Like the ones in my hot chocolate?"

"I don't know what that is," I responded.

"You know." She sat me on her lap and gestured with her hands as she said, "It's really warm chocolate, my mom puts milk in mines. And there are a bunch of tiny marshmallows that I drink."

Hearing her say she ate my kind, made my stomach sink, and my heart break. I thought I'd found someone that treated marshmallows like living beings. But she was no different than the monsters who murdered my siblings. I lowered my head and began to walk away.

She grabbed me by my head and sat me back on the palm of her hand. "Where are you going?"

She raised me to her ear and I said, "I don't want to be eaten."

She gasped. "Oh no! I won't eat you!"

"But you eat marshmallows. All marshmallows are like me. To my knowledge, I'm just the only one who can walk. We talk just like you, I have a mom like you, I used to have a house like…well, similar to yours, but I was taken away to be eaten by humans." I paced back and forth on her palm. "I left a home because I want to survive and find a home to call my own. I want to feel safe every day of my life. So I can't be friends with or talk to you, because you eat people like me."

The young girl panicked, and I mean panicked, she stumbled over her words and looked from side to side. "I-I won't eat any more marshmallows ever again! I promise! You can live with me and my family. We'll be your forever home."

I sat down on her hand and crossed my arms. I had to think about it carefully. After the last home gave me a false sense of security, I couldn't take that risk. But the sincerity in her eyes, told me that I should trust her.

I nodded and said, "Okay. Only if you promise your family won't eat me."

"I swear on my Bratz dolls." She lifted her left hand in the air and nodded. She looked at her pink watch and said, "The school bus will be here in like 5 minutes."

She stood up and ran to the side of her house. She stacked a bunch of sticks and leaves in a pile with a cover over the top and continued, "I can't take you to school, but you should stay here 'til I get back. Okay?"

"Okay," I shouted. I crawled under the thingy and sat down.

I peeked out and watched her run back to the spot she sat in, and a yellow monster filled with human children arrived and she climbed into its mouth. I thought it was weird, but as I got older, I learned it was called a "school bus."

When she returned from school, hoooours later, she carried me into her home to her bedroom. She gave me her dollhouse to live in. It had a nice bed, and kitchen. We spent time talking about what happened to me, well most of what happened to me. I learned her name, but at the time, she wanted to be called Lilly.

Lilly kept me a secret from her family until her mom found me in her room one day. She thought I was a toy and questioned where Lilly had taken me from. But Lilly was adamant about proving I was a real, talking being. Her mom lifted me to her ear, and I gave the speech I gave Lilly the first day I met her.

Her mom freaked out for a bit, but after some time, she was able to accept that I was a living being. She threw away all traces of the dead, dried marshmallow carcasses in their home, especially the hot chocolate. And even gave me my own room in their guest room. Of course when they had guests, I was kept a secret and my room was given to them. But it was worth it. I had a safe space.

Her mom made me clothes for me so Lilly and I could match. She used tiny fabrics. I loved wearing hats the most. She made me all kinds of outfits, and even pajamas to wear.

Lilly(6) and I (5 months), playing with mom's camera and our feather boas.

The only time that I didn't feel safe, was when her brothers tried to eat me, arguing that I was no different from cows and other animals they ate. But Lilly was there to protect me. Or when their cats thought I was a toy and chased me around the house. Lilly and her…our mom, protected me. The only thing I needed was a name.

None of us were creative enough. And my new family always just called me "little marshmallow." So my adoptive mom decided my name would be Marsh Mallow. I thought it was a fitting name. And it gave me an identity.

# Chapter Six
## A New Beginning

I lived with my family. I stayed in the house until I was 18. Being the youngest, they were always protective of me. And they knew if others found out that I was a sentient marshmallow, they would come after me. But I wanted to do something with my life. Seeing the human world through the TV, my desire to be something intensified. I convinced my mom to let me enroll in online school. She reluctantly agreed and my journey to an education started.

I had the highest grades, even higher than my human siblings. My mother said she never chose favorites, but I could always tell there was some bias against me. I mean, to her I was a cute little talking marshmallow. I started school later than my siblings but I excelled in everything. I could hear her nagging them about their grades and that a little marshmallow like me shouldn't have better grades. Especially because I still didn't know what grass was nor how it worked at the time.

But that just gave me the motivation to strive for my mom to approve of me and think of me as more than just a little naïve marshmallow that didn't know what things were.

With Lilly to help me study, my grades were even better. I skipped many grades and by 18, I could graduate online high school. Hey didn't know I was a marshmallow, so they were appalled when I went to the graduation. I was insecure with all the stares, but my family was reassuring. I walked, well Lilly carried me, so we walked across the stage, and she grabbed my diploma for me, and I shouted as best I could into the mic, "Whoo! This Marsh Mallow graduated high school!"

My family cheered and soon, most of the students and parents clapped.

Me with my high school diploma and cap.

I think the craziest part after that was that the videos the students took of me went viral. My mom's biggest fear. She received call after call about what I was and how I was able to move and talk. I had numerous interviews and people trying to eat me.

The publicity did help though. I applied for Harvard and Yale, and was accepted into Harvard. Lilly was 6 years older than me, so she had already graduated college. She helped me navigate the school safely, and defended me against any bullying. Attending the school, I wasn't sure what I would major in, but I wanted to raise awareness to stop the slaughter of marshmallows. I created the term Marsh People to refer to my fellow marshmallows.

I majored in social studies. And dedicated my time to speaking about my experiences as a Marsh Person. Soon a troupe of marshmatarians banded together to join my cause of ending the need to eat Marsh People. It became a huge online debate, and very disgruntled people asking why they had to give up something they loved in order to make Marsh People comfortable.

With donations from my supporters, I created support spaces for Marsh People, which consisted of large building with different sections for each shape of Marsh People to live. They rolled around the buildings, making friends, and getting a second chance at life.

I wasn't sure why I was the only one who could walk and had arms, but that's why I decided to let scientists do some tests on me to figure out why I was the only Marsh Person that could walk.

The results were inconclusive. A true miracle they believed. Which they expressed to me many times was the only reason they could believe a miracle was something that could exist.

But I thought about it in my alone time. The environment, my condition, what I'd eaten, and then I decided to give something a try. I took willing participants to the local landfill, with the protection of marshmatarians against the fur demons that murdered my sister, and sat them under the large thing similar to the one I was under. We had them eat the pink sticky stuff, which I learned was gum, a wad each and left them alone for 2 weeks. When we came back, they had sprouted legs. It didn't make sense to me, but I didn't care. I had discovered the way to give my fellow Marsh People limbs.

We proceeded to give willing Marsh People limbs and it improved their lives. I was making a difference I would never have been able to do if I had given up in that kitchen, 20 some years ago.

# Chapter Seven
## Where I am now

What us Marsh People are, is still unknown to the world, it turned out that only locals knew about us. The videos of me were thought to be CGI and people pushed the phenomenon to the back of their minds.

At one of the facilities I created for Marsh People, a young Marsh man approached me to tell me his story. It was somewhat similar to my experience and we had a connection. His name was Mark Mellow. He asked me out to dinner and it was the best night of my life.

After a month of dating, Mark proposed to me. My family thought I was rushing our relationship. But even humans couldn't find their soulmates, let alone a partner who truly cared about them. It was even more taboo for Marsh People to find love. So, I said yes, and with my family's help, had a lovely wedding.

Our wedding was one of the best moments of my life. It was tricky setting up a wedding for two Marsh People. Everything was too big for us, Lilly had to make a bouquet out of craft supplies and many couldn't hear us. They set a mic just in front of us, so the pastor could hear. We said our vows and he handed me a very tiny ring from a toy.

Our wedding photo. We had to stand very close to the camera to be seen. We had fruits and vegetables at the reception and every attendee was respectful of us and the many Marsh People that attended. I will say one horrific thing happened. One person did snatch a Marsh Person and ate them. But we took care of that human swiftly.

Other than that, it was an amazing wedding. I love Mark with all my heart. I wish for us to safely spend the rest of our lives together.

We're now expecting a shipment of Marsh Children to my condo that I share with my husband, and Lilly. It's an exciting moment and I can't wait to see my little bundles of joy!

And as a mother, like any other, I want my children to grow up in a world where they won't be eaten. They can go to school like human children and become a Harvard graduates like me.

So now, I am trying again to end the killing of Marsh People all over the world.

Please, if you have read this far in my book, understand that we are sentient beings just like you. We may be smaller than you and you might think we taste good, but look at the bigger picture and give those Marsh People in your cabinets and pantries, a chance to be something great.

Do the right thing, and raise them like your own children.

If you have an inspirational story about yourself as a marshmallow or any adopted marsh children, please email them to:

marshpeoplearepeopletoo@gmail.com

I will share the inspirational stories to my new twitter account. Something I didn't know existed until Lilly told me about it. My username is: @Marshmallowslo

Pictures of me and my family

Mark and I's, first time at a pool. Learned our lesson.

Gardening with mom

Thanksgiving, 2020. Me, my third older brother, Lilly, and my dad.

My eldest brother and I. My first Christmas with my family

My first Christmas with Mark

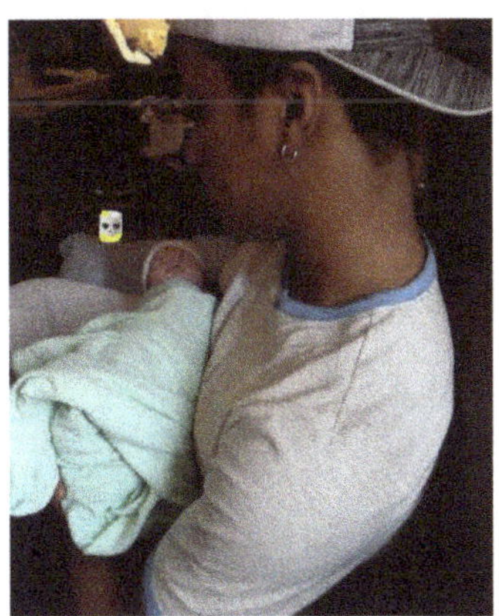

Meeting my nephew in 2017.
My second oldest brother and I

# About the Author

Marsh Mallow is the mother of 16 marsh children. They live in Madison, WI with their husband Mark and sister Lilly. They have opened Marsh facilities across the United States for Marsh People to find safe spaces to live their lives. They have helped over 1 million Marsh People walk.

Their dream is to expand their facilities abroad and save Marsh People everywhere in the world.

# Dedication

Dedicated to my siblings, and my mother.

Dedicated to the many people who helped me on my journey of survival and finding my forever home.